I'm on each spread. Can you find me?

Think Fair Trade First!

Created by Ingrid Hess

Edited by Sam Carpenter

FAIR TRADE RESOURCE NETWORK

education and discussion to make trade fair

Ingrid Hess

Think Fair Trade First

Library of Congress Cataloging in-Publication Data
Hess, Ingrid
Think Fair Trade First / Created by Ingrid Hess; Edited by Sam Carpenter
            p. cm.
      ISBN 13 –   978-0-615-34337-2
      ISBN 10 -   0-615-34337-6

Library of Congress Control Number: 2010920754

To order or request information please visit www.ftrn.org or call 917.464.5558.

For Lindsey Blake, who's been a Fair Trade volunteer since the age of 8,

&

For all the Fair Trade producers & supporters who help make the world a better place.

One Saturday afternoon Aunt Mabel picked up Stella and Henry. She was taking them shopping for a birthday gift for their mother.

Every day people all over the world buy the things they need. They buy food and clothes and gifts and toys.

Have you ever wondered where the things you buy come from?

Well, somewhere in the world someone makes the things you buy. After they make the product it travels to a store where you can buy it.

This journey that begins with the person who makes the product and ends at the store where you can buy the product is called the supply chain.

The supply chain has many links. Each link is another step that gets the product closer to the store. For example, the boat that sails across the ocean with the product in it is a link. Or the person who delivers the products to the store is a link. A supply chain is necessary for you to get the things you buy.

"Where are we going?" asked Henry.

"We're are going to a Fair Trade store," said Aunt Mabel.

"What's that?" asked Stella.

"It's a store where good things happen when you make purchases," said Aunt Mabel.

"What do you mean?" asked Henry.

"You'll see," said Aunt Mabel and she headed toward town.

The two children were very curious.

Unfortunately, many times some people along the supply chain make lots of money and become rich while other people along the supply chain make little money and are poor.

This isn't fair.

Also, many times the Earth isn't taken care of properly when products are being made. Trees are cut down, water is polluted and land is destroyed.

This isn't fair.

When people are poor and the Earth is being destroyed, it is very difficult for them to be happy and healthy. Is there anything we can do to make the supply chain better?

YES!

After a while Aunt Mabel stopped the car.

"We're here," she said.

Stella and Henry jumped out of the car and followed her into the store.

What is Fair Trade?

Fair Trade is a way of selling things that makes sure every person who is part of the supply chain is treated with dignity and respect. When people are treated with dignity and respect they can have much better lives. For a product to become Fair Trade there are eight principles that guide people's work along the chain. These principles are all about caring for people.

The Fair Trade store was different from any store that Stella and Henry had ever seen. It was full of beautiful things from all over the world. They saw teapots from Vietnam, instruments from Cameroon, chimes from the Philippines, and baskets from Bangladesh. Stella and Henry started looking around for the perfect present for their mother.

The 8 principles of Fair Trade are:

- Creating jobs for people who aren't usually hired
- Caring for the environment
- Capacity building
- Paying a fair price
- Giving women & girls the same opportunities as men & boys
- Building sustainable long-term relationships
- Supporting good working conditions
- Educating people about Fair Trade & encouraging them to get involved

Let's look at each principle more closely.

Stella picked up a woven bag.

"Aunt Mabel," she said, "Remember how you told us that good things happen when people buy things from Fair Trade stores?"

"Yes," said Aunt Mabel.

"Well, what good thing will happen if I buy this purse?"

Aunt Mabel looked at the purse Stella was holding. "This purse is made by people in India who have a disease called leprosy. Many people with this disease become crippled and can't find work. Fair Trade organizations employ people with leprosy and other diseases so they can have better lives. When you buy this purse, people who have trouble being hired get jobs."

Creating jobs for people who aren't usually hired

In many countries people who have physical and mental disabilities, those who aren't educated and women have a very hard time getting a job. Fair Trade organizations often hire these people so they can have better lives.

Fair Trade Fact

Over 7.5 million disadvantaged producers and their families are benefiting from Fair Trade.

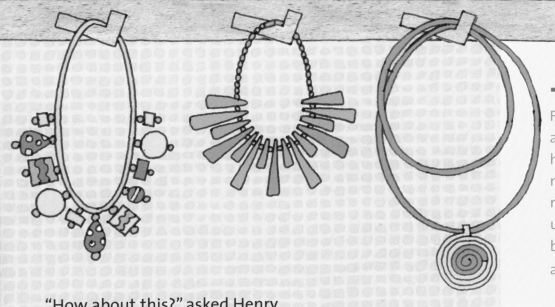

Fair Trade products are made and shipped in ways that don't hurt the Earth. Using recycled materials, replanting trees to replace wood that is used and using organically grown and biodegradable packing materials are common Fair Trade practices.

"How about this?" asked Henry.

Aunt Mabel looked at the piece of jewelry in his hand.

"This necklace is made in Kenya," she said. "The beads are made of recycled magazines. Fair Trade artists use earth-friendly practices in their products. When you buy this and other Fair Trade products, you help the planet because recycling cuts down on pollution, keeps water cleaner and helps preserve natural resources."

Fair Trade Fact

More than 1 billion people have no access to clean water.

Stella and Henry were excited about helping the planet. They ran to find other gifts. Stella came back with a soup mix.

"This Fair Trade product is made in the United States," said Aunt Mabel. "Fair Trade helps the women who make these soup mixes learn business skills. They receive computer training, learn about money management and budgeting, and develop interviewing skills. Fair Trade artists all over the world learn skills that help them become self-sufficient. When you buy this soup mix you are helping people become independent."

Capacity building

Fair Trade organizations do more than just buy products. They also teach producers how to set up their businesses, understand the marketplace and be independent. They give producers information about how products are selling and teach them how to invest in their business so they can create even more good jobs.

The two children rushed off to find more goodies. They came back with bags of Colombian coffee.

"Buying Fair Trade coffee is very important," said Aunt Mabel. "It is the most popular Fair Trade product."

"Coffee?" said Stella. "I think chocolate should be the most popular Fair Trade product."

"Me too," said Henry.

Aunt Mabel smiled. "Both coffee and chocolate are important. When coffee and cocoa farmers are paid a fair price, they can afford food, shelter, medicine and education. Fair Trade organizations help farmers set fair prices for their products. When you buy Fair Trade coffee and chocolate, you ensure that the producers are getting the money they deserve."

4

Paying a fair price

Fair Trade organizations work with producers to determine a fair price that values their work and helps them live a decent life. Many Fair Traders pay for their order promptly. Most other importers wait 60-90 days before paying, making it hard for small producers to survive. Fair Traders are open about how they do business, so you can ask them about how they determine what is fair.

Fair Trade Fact

For every $3.00 cup of non-Fair Trade coffee sold, farmers receive 2 cents.

One more time the two children went to find a treasure. They returned with their hands full of finger puppets.

Aunt Mabel said, "Did you know that in many places around the world, boys go to school but girls don't?"

Stella and Henry shook their heads.

"These finger puppets are made in Nepal. Many women artists who work in Fair Trade in Nepal and in other countries around the world are able to earn enough money to send both their sons and their

daughters to school. When you buy these finger puppets and other Fair Trade products, you are helping many girls get an education."

⑤

Giving women & girls the same opportunities as men & boys

There are many countries where women and girls don't have as many opportunities as men and boys. Fair Trade makes sure to give jobs to as many women as possible. Most of the people who make Fair Trade items are women. When women are treated with the same dignity and respect as men, everyone in the community benefits.

"What about this?" asked Henry, holding up a brightly colored shirt.

"This shirt was made in Ghana," said Aunt Mabel. "Some women dye the fabric and other women sew the dyed fabric into clothes. Instead of just buying products from these women one time, Fair Trade organizations keep coming back to place more orders. Continued orders provide the artists with a steady income. When people have a steady income, they are able to plan for their future. When you buy this shirt, you are helping women in Ghana plan for their future."

⑥ Building sustainable, long-term relationships

Fair Trade organizations build long-term partnerships with producers. Because of these stable relationships the producers can count on orders and make long-term plans for their businesses.

Fair Trade Fact

One of the areas in which Fair Trade goods are rapidly expanding in recent years is clothing and cotton items.

Stella and Henry looked around and saw a beautiful wall hanging.

"Does this tree help too?" they asked.

Aunt Mabel smiled. "Oh yes. This lovely wall hanging was made in Haiti. In many parts of the world, including Haiti, people are forced to work very long hours in dirty, dangerous work places. People who work

It is very important that people work in good conditions. All work sites must be safe and clean, no children are exploited and no slaves are used. If you buy something Fair Trade, you can be sure that the people who made it are being treated with dignity and respect.

in Fair Trade have clean, safe places to work and aren't forced to work long hours. Fair Trade helps more kids go to school and have a chance to play. No children are taken advantage of with Fair Trade. When you buy this wall hanging you help artisans have a safe, clean and fair work environment."

Fair Trade Fact

It is estimated that 158 million children between the ages of 5 to 14 are involved in child labor around the world.

"Is there any way that kids can help Fair Trade without having to buy things?" asked Stella.

Everyone along the supply chain needs to tell people about Fair Trade and how important it is. People need to be encouraged to get involved. Volunteers are always needed. The more that people get involved with Fair Trade, the more producers and their families all over the world will live better lives.

"Absolutely," said Aunt Mabel. "Children are important for Fair Trade to succeed. Most people don't know what Fair Trade is, so children can help to spread the word."

Fair Trade Fact

Stories about producers are often attached to Fair Trade items. This is a great way to get to know about people involved in Fair Trade.

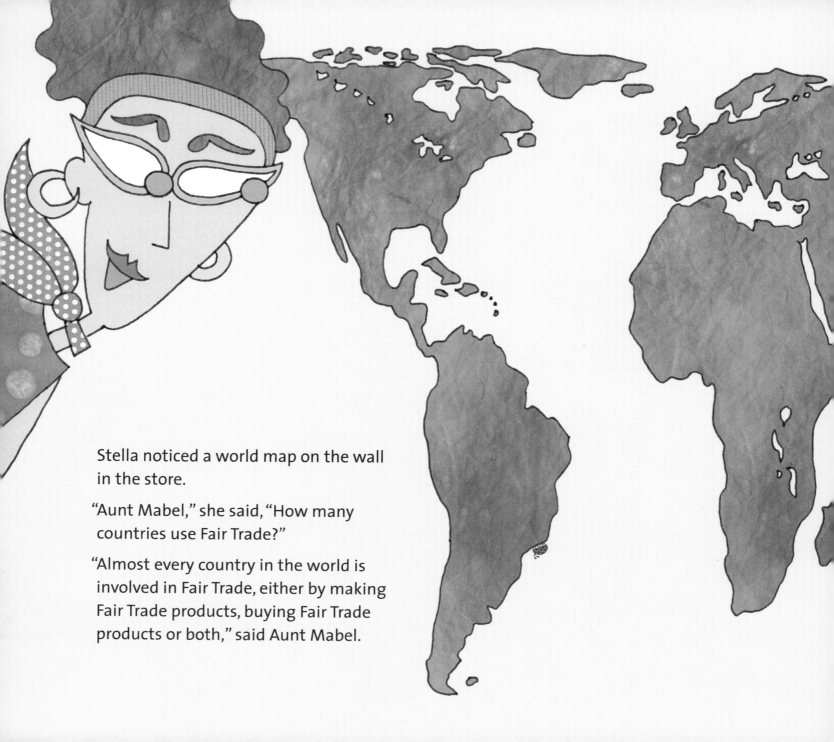

Stella noticed a world map on the wall in the store.

"Aunt Mabel," she said, "How many countries use Fair Trade?"

"Almost every country in the world is involved in Fair Trade, either by making Fair Trade products, buying Fair Trade products or both," said Aunt Mabel.

It's everywhere!

Many countries are involved in the Fair Trade movement. When Fair Trade first began, countries in the South made the products and people in the North bought them. This is no longer the case. Now Fair Trade producers are all over the world and buyers of Fair Trade products are all over the world.

"Does this store sell all the Fair Trade things in the world?" asked Henry.

"Oh no," said Aunt Mabel. "There are many products that are Fair Trade. This store carries just a few of them."

What products are available Fair Trade?

All kinds of things are available Fair Trade. Here are just a few examples of what is available:

- bananas
- pottery
- games
- clothing
- coffee
- instruments
- cards
- kites
- mobiles
- chocolate
- rice
- mittens
- ornaments
- paper weights
- footballs
- candlesticks
- dishes
- bookends
- furniture
- lamps
- jewelry
- baskets
- soap
- purses
- tea
- toys
- jewelry boxes
- wall hangings

Soon it was time to leave. Stella and Henry decided on some flowers from South Africa that were made from recycled aluminum cans. A volunteer wrapped their gift.

How can a person tell if a product is Fair Trade?

The easiest way to know if a product is Fair Trade is to buy it in a Fair Trade store. When you buy something in one of these stores you know that it is Fair Trade. You can visit www.fairtradefederation.org to find a Fair Trade store or look for this logo where you shop.

The second way is to look for the Fair Trade label. If a product has the Fair Trade label you know it has followed most of the 8 principles in this book. If you want to learn more about how a product becomes Fair Trade certified and earns the Fair Trade label, visit www.transfairusa.org.

Think Fair Trade First!

Think Fair Trade First!

As they walked to the car, Stella said, "Fair Trade seems like a great thing."

"It is," said Aunt Mabel.

"How do we know when to buy something Fair Trade?" asked Henry.

"Well," said Aunt Mabel, "when you need to buy something see if it is available Fair Trade. If it is, then consider buying it."

"So really what you are saying is, Think Fair Trade First," said Stella.

"Yeah, Think Fair Trade First," Henry giggled.

"Exactly," said Aunt Mabel.

Think Fair Trade First!

Kids make a difference!

Here are three easy ways that you can become involved.

Spread the word

Now that you know about Fair Trade you can help explain it to others. Tell your parents, your grandparents, your teachers and your friends. Encourage people to buy Fair Trade.

Volunteer

Some Fair Trade stores need volunteers. Volunteers unpack boxes of new products, tell customers about Fair Trade and sell things. You and a grown-up can volunteer together.

Organize a sale

You can organize a Fair Trade sale at your school or your place of worship. Contact the nearest Fair Trade store to find out how.

And with that, they headed back home with the perfect gift for their mother and lots of new knowledge to share.

Remember: Think Fair Trade First. You can make a difference!

Acknowledgements

The creation of this book was possible due to the generosity of many Fair Trade groups. These include:

ACP

Fair Trade Federation

Fair Trade Resource Network

Global Gifts

Global Mamas

Mahaguthi

Mai Handicrafts

M.E.S.H.

SERRV

Soup of Success

Tara Projects

Ten Thousand Villages

Also special thanks to The University of Notre Dame for supporting this research.

Ingrid Hess teaches graphic design at the University of Notre Dame. She is a graduate of Goshen College in Indiana and trained in Fine Arts at Indiana University in Bloomington. She wrote her masters thesis on Ten Thousand Villages in 1996 and has been involved with the Fair Trade movement ever since.

Sam Carpenter serves as executive director of Global Gifts, a nonprofit Fair Trade organization with stores in Central Indiana. Sam serves on the board of the Fair Trade Resource Network and was its chair in 2009. Sam was recognized with the Indianapolis Business Journal's 2010 "40 Under 40" award for his work with Global Gifts and Fair Trade. Sam wrote his master's thesis on the subject of Fair Trade in 2000.

Fair Trade Resource Network (www.ftrn.org) seeks to improve people's lives through Fair Trade alternatives by providing information, leadership, and inspiration. FTRN gathers, develops, and disseminates educational resources to organizations and people interested in the movement to build a more just and sustainable world through Fair Trade.